Kenai

Denahi

Sitka

Rutt

Tuke

D1145251

© 2011 Disney Enterprises, Inc.
Published by Hachette Partworks Ltd
ISBN: 978-1-906965-53-2
Date of Printing: March 2011
Printed in Singapore by Tien Wah Press

Disney

H hachette

Long ago, there lived three
brothers who were taught that
the lights of the northern
sky were the spirits of their
ancestors. These spirits had
the power to make changes
– small things into big,
winter into spring, and
boys into men...

One day, the villagers gathered for a special ceremony. Tanana, the shaman woman, presented Kenai, the youngest of the three brothers, with his totem – the ancient symbol he was to follow to become a man.

"Your totem is love," said Tanana, giving him a carved bear totem. "Let love guide your actions, and one day you will place your mark next to those of our ancestors," she added, pointing to a wall covered with handprints.

"The bear of love?" Kenai frowned. "Wanna trade?" he asked his brothers.

His older brothers laughed. They had
already received their totems. Sitka's was the
eagle of guidance and Denahi's was the wolf
of wisdom.

After the ceremony, the brothers left to get
the fish they had caught for the evening's
feast. "A bear doesn't love anyone," Kenai
said unhappily to Sitka. "They don't think,
they don't feel, they're..."

Just then, Denahi found the remains of the
basket that had held their fish.

"... thieves!" shouted Kenai, staring at the
bear tracks.

Kenai followed the tracks into the woods to find the basket.

When Kenai didn't return, Sitka and Denahi went after him. It wasn't long before they heard Kenai cry out. He had slipped off a ledge trying to escape from a bear!

Quickly, Denahi distracted the bear while Sitka helped Kenai. But then Denahi slipped into a dangerous crevice. While Kenai helped him, Sitka faced the bear.

Suddenly, the bear turned and headed for Kenai and Denahi. To save his brothers, Sitka raised his spear and thrust it down into a crack in the ice. The ice split, and the piece on which Sitka and the bear were standing plunged into the freezing water below.

From far above, Kenai and Denahi saw the bear emerge from the water – but not Sitka. Their oldest brother would now be joining the Great Spirits in the form of his totem, the eagle. Denahi felt great sadness. But Kenai felt great anger!

The next day, Kenai was determined to go after the bear that had caused Sitka's death. But Denahi would not go with him. Angry, Kenai threw his bear totem into a fire and left the village.

Tanana pulled the totem from the fire.

"I've got to go after him," Denahi said, taking the bear totem.

Kenai tracked and eventually found the bear. After a fierce struggle, Kenai fell to the ground. The animal charged towards him. Kenai raised his spear. The bear crashed into him, let out a roar, then fell silent.

Suddenly, lights burst down
from the sky and swirled around
Kenai. A giant eagle landed
next to him and turned into
Sitka. Then Kenai felt himself
being lifted into the air. He
didn't realise that he was being
magically transformed into the
creature he hated most – a bear!

The lights disappeared and it
began to rain.

Just then, Denahi arrived and saw a grizzly bear standing on Kenai's clothes. Denahi didn't know that Kenai was now a bear. He thought that the bear had killed Kenai. Before he could react, a bolt of lightning sent the bear tumbling into the river below. Kenai was swept away.

Now it was Denahi's turn to seek revenge. He tied Kenai's totem to his spear and began to track the bear.

When Kenai opened his eyes the next morning, Tanana was leaning over him.

Kenai spoke to her excitedly, telling her all that had happened to him. But all Tanana could hear was growling!

"Kenai, I don't speak bear!" said the wise woman.

Kenai didn't understand. Then he looked into the river at his reflection.

"No!" he shouted. He twisted around and looked at his furry tail.

"*AAAAARGH*!" he cried.

To get Kenai's attention, Tanana took off her boot and bonked him on the head with it.

"Listen to me! Sitka did this!" said Tanana. "Take it up with your brother's spirit. If you want to change, go to the mountain where the lights touch the earth. He'll help you make up for what you've done wrong."

Kenai was shocked. "But... I didn't do anything wrong," he began. But Tanana had already disappeared.

Kenai didn't know where
to go, and he had no one to
ask – until he heard two chipmunks
talking. Kenai was surprised he could
understand them. He tried to talk to them, but
the terrified chipmunks raced away.

Then Kenai heard a family of geese flying
overhead.

"Are we there yet?" a young goose asked his
father.

Kenai frantically tried asking for directions
to where the lights touch the
earth, but the geese
kept flying.

Two moose brothers named Rutt and Tuke were watching Kenai.

"What's he getting all worked up about?" said Tuke.

"Maybe the goose pooped on him, eh?" laughed Rutt.

But the moose stopped laughing when they saw the bear was heading straight for them.

"How's it going, bear?" asked Tuke, a little nervously.

"I'm not a bear. I hate bears," answered Kenai.

"Well gee, you're one big beaver!" said Rutt.

"I'm NOT a beaver! I'm a bear. No, I mean I'm not a bear, I'm a man!" shouted Kenai. "I was transformed into a bear. Magically."

The moose thought Kenai was crazy, but decided to play along.

"Oh yeah, we're not moose either. We're... squirrels," Tuke offered.

"Why am I even talking to a couple of dumb moose?" Kenai wondered, as he stomped off.

Almost immediately, Kenai's foot
was caught in a trap. He swung in the
air from one leg, struggling to get free.
    A bear cub named Koda stepped
out of the bushes and offered to help
Kenai. But Kenai didn't want help
from a bear – especially from a chatty
little cub like Koda.

Kenai tried to free himself, but it was no use. And Koda just wouldn't leave.

"Don't you have somewhere to go?" asked Kenai.

"Yeah, the Salmon Run," replied Koda. "How about this? I get you down, then we go together?"

Kenai was so exhausted that he agreed to go to the
Salmon Run if Koda freed him.

With that, Koda sprang the trap and Kenai
crashed to the ground.

Just then, Koda sniffed
the air. He could smell
an approaching hunter!
"Run!" he cried, as he
scampered off.

The hunter was Denahi!

Kenai cried, "Denahi,
it's me – Kenai!"

But all Denahi
heard was growling.
To Denahi, this was
the bear that had killed
Kenai. He threw his spear,
but missed.

Kenai realised that Denahi
was hunting him, and ran away.

Kenai ducked into the ice cave where Koda was hiding. Kenai told the little bear that he wasn't going to go to the Salmon Run.

So Koda told Kenai the truth: a hunter had caused Koda and his mother to be separated. Koda's only hope of finding her was to go to the Salmon Run. Still, Kenai refused to go.

"C'mon, please? Every night we watch the lights touch the mountain," pleaded Koda.

"You're kidding me!" said Kenai excitedly. That was the place where he could be changed back into a man! Kenai agreed to go with the little cub.

The next morning, the two bears set out.
At first, Kenai was annoyed by
Koda's constant chatter and silly
games. But after a while,
Kenai joined in and even
had some fun.

Once again, Rutt and Tuke appeared. "There's a hunter followin' us," Rutt explained. The two moose wanted the bears to protect them.

Kenai knew that the hunter was Denahi. And he had a plan to keep Denahi from following their tracks. The group, along with some other animals, found a herd of mammoths and hitched a ride on their backs.

That night, as they watched the lights in the northern sky, Koda said, "Mom says the spirits make magical changes in the world."

"My brother Sitka is a spirit," explained Kenai. "If it wasn't for him, I wouldn't be here." Then he added, "He was killed by a monster."

Koda looked up at the lights and said, "Thanks, Sitka. If it weren't for you, I would never have met Kenai." Then Koda said to Kenai, "I always wanted a brother." Touched, Kenai let the cub sleep next to him.

The next morning, the two bears headed off by themselves. They came to a cave covered with paintings. As they looked at one picture of a hunter facing a fierce bear, Koda said, "Those monsters are really scary – especially with those sticks."

Kenai was shocked to learn that Koda saw humans as monsters. Kenai had thought the bears were the monsters, but now he wasn't sure what he believed.

Later, the two bears came to a valley with spurting geysers. Koda remembered that the Salmon Run was just on the other side. As they made their way through the valley, the little bear was as playful as ever. But suddenly, Koda stopped playing.

THWACK! A spear just missed Kenai by inches! Denahi had found them!

Kenai grabbed Koda and rushed towards a log bridge. They were halfway across the bridge when Denahi cut the log loose. Kenai tossed Koda up to safe ground, then scrambled to safety just as the bridge collapsed.

Denahi screamed in rage as the bears got away. When Kenai looked back, he felt very sad that his brother did not know him.

Before long, Kenai and Koda reached the
Salmon Run. At first, Kenai was scared
to be among the huge bears. But they
were friendly and welcomed him as
part of the family.

Kenai began to learn how to fish, just like the other bears.

Although Koda was sad to learn that his mother wasn't there yet, he was happy to be with his bear pals again.

Soon, Kenai and Koda were having fun.

Later in the day, the bears gathered around to tell stories of what they had done in the past year. Kenai explained that he'd been on the hardest journey of his life with the biggest pain in the neck he had ever met. "But what do you expect from a little brother?" Kenai added, looking at Koda.

Then it was Koda's turn. He told a story of his mother protecting him from some hunters. She and one of the hunters had plunged into the river when the hunter had cracked the ice.

Kenai couldn't believe what he was hearing. Koda was telling the story of the day his brother Sitka was killed by a bear. Now he knew it was also the story of a mother bear protecting her cub.

"She got out of the water OK," continued Koda. "That's how we got separated. Right after that, I met Kenai."

Hearing this, Kenai realised that the bear he had killed was Koda's mother! Kenai felt terrible.

Kenai felt so bad that he ran away. But Koda finally found him. Kenai knew he had to tell the cub the truth.

"Koda," Kenai began, "I have a story to tell you... it's mostly about a monster." Then Kenai explained that he had done something very wrong. "Your mother's not coming back," he finished sadly.

Overwhelmed by the news, Koda ran away from Kenai.

Having no way to make things better, Kenai began to climb the mountain where the lights touch the earth.

After he reached the top, Kenai called for Sitka. A strange figure moved towards Kenai. It was Denahi! But Denahi did not see his brother Kenai. What he saw was a bear on whom he had sworn revenge. Denahi ran at Kenai with his spear.

Just then, Koda came charging
to protect Kenai. The little cub
had decided to follow Kenai after
all. He knocked into Denahi and
ran off with his spear. Denahi
angrily took off after Koda.

"Leave him alone!" roared
Kenai, risking his own life to
protect Koda.

Suddenly, there was a huge
flash of light.

A great eagle
appeared and picked
Kenai off the ground.
Magical lights
began to swirl. Kenai
was a human once
again. Denahi was
confused and amazed.
The bear he had just
been trying to kill was
his brother!

The eagle spirit of Sitka had turned Kenai into a bear to help him learn his gift of love. As a bear, Kenai had just shown deep love for Koda. He was willing to give his own life to protect him.

Awestruck, Kenai looked down at his human body as Sitka changed from an eagle to his human spirit form.

Then Kenai spotted
a terrified Koda hiding
behind a boulder.

"Koda, don't be afraid,"
said Kenai. "It's me."

Denahi placed the bear totem around Kenai's neck. The totem reminded Kenai that little Koda needed someone to protect him. "He needs me," Kenai explained to his brothers. He wanted to be a bear again.

"It's all right," said Denahi. "No matter what you choose, you will always be my little brother."

The two brothers embraced.
Then, with a burst of swirling
light, Sitka turned Kenai
back into a bear again.

Denahi looked up
at his brother,
who was now
an enormous
bear. "Did I
say *little*?" he
exclaimed.

Then Kenai,
Denahi and
Koda watched
the sky as Sitka
turned back into an
eagle. He flew back into the
magical lights to join the Great Spirits.

It was time for another ceremony in the village. It was Kenai's turn to put his mark on the ceremonial wall to prove that he had learned the way of his totem and was now an adult.

With Koda and the villagers watching, Denahi helped Kenai place his pawprint on the wall among the handprints of his ancestors.

The pawprint would help future
generations remember this tale of
love and brotherhood.